The Greenwood

Nathaniel Baker

Published by Nathaniel Baker, 2024.

This is a work of fiction. Similarities to real people, places, or events are entirely coincidental.

THE GREENWOOD

First edition. February 10, 2024.

Copyright © 2024 Nathaniel Baker.

ISBN: 979-8224301829

Written by Nathaniel Baker.

The

Greenwood

Catherine was deep in sleep, lost in a strange dream. It started in a dark, eerie forest. The atmosphere in this dream world was dense, almost palpable, with an otherworldly weight. The shadows danced, and the wind whispered spooky secrets through the twisted trees. It felt heavy and strange.

Then, the dream changed. An old trailer was in the middle of the spooky woods, and inside, a massive fire was burning everything. The wind moaned like it was sad about something.

Suddenly, the dark forest lit up with fireflies. They tried to glow, but the fire inside the trailer was too intense. The fire spread wildly, transforming the once mysterious woods into a chilling and scary place.

A haunting sight awaited Catherine in the trailer—a human figure whose skin looked burnt. It was a creepy sight. An unsettling image that added to the bizarre nature of her dream.

All of a sudden, Catherine woke up. Found herself in the dark room, beads of sweat glistening on her forehead. The clock on her phone displayed an eerie 3:33 in the morning. Her lock screen, a picture of her and her daughter Ava, projected an image of happiness, a stark contrast to the lingering unease from the dream.

The peaceful facade of the dream was shattered when Ava, Catherine's eleven-year-old daughter, appeared in the doorway. She, too, had been disturbed by a nightmare involving the pursuit of twelve clowns. Catherine, a mother accustomed to the unique needs of her daughter, comforted her, asking if she wanted to sleep in the safety of her bed and away from the spooky dreams.

Ava, nodding in agreement, approached the bed with measured caution. Her actions, a curious routine that involved circling the bed and occasionally testing the duvet, reflected a careful attempt to understand her surroundings. Catherine observed this with a lingering sadness, an emotion that only a parent of a child with special needs could genuinely understand.

Ava finished her usual dance, a funny one that made her feel better, then got into bed and lay down on the side without anyone. Catherine was torn between the desire for comfort and the awareness of Ava's need for space. Thinking intently about it, she refrained from attempting physical contact. Instead, she rolled over, hugging the edge of the bed as silent sobs betrayed her emotions, lulling her into a restless sleep.

The sun timidly peeked through the curtains, casting a warm glow on the simple kitchen where Ava sat at the table, nibbling on toast with carefully cut-off crusts. At the same time, Catherine was immersed in the daily ritual of preparing for another day of responsibilities. She wore the dual expressions of efficiency and weariness. This expression clearly defined the life of a working mother.

The rhythmic sounds of a car honking outside disrupted their morning routine, letting them know the arrival of John, Ava's father. This abrupt interruption pushed Catherine into hastening up. She told Ava to get ready for school, but Ava wanted her mom to take her, as it was a Tuesday tradition. This was a predictable behaviour of children with special needs, anchored with her familiarity of the weekly schedule.

"Tuesday is my day, Mom," Ava asserted, a small but significant rebellion against the disruption of their established routine. The persistent honking outside mirrored Ava's protest.

Tired and frustrated, Catherine told Ava to get in the car. This led to Ava rocking back and forth, a physical manifestation of the emotional turbulence within.

Feeling sorry for her outburst, Catherine knelt beside Ava, asking her to follow instructions. Ava, in a robotic way, picked up her bag and went to the door. John was there, acknowledging the disruption but proposing a treat of double chocolate ice cream after school. The promise swayed Ava, and, with a nod of agreement, she reluctantly agreed to step into the waiting car.

As the car pulled away from the curb, Catherine stood at the doorway, her eyes following the vehicle until it disappeared. What she felt was more than just physical tiredness. It was the tiredness that comes from being a mom in a world that needs both routine and flexibility.

Her face etched with the remnants of her earlier disagreement with John, Catherine embarked on her daily commute to London. The train, crowded with faces absorbed in their worlds, mirrored the mundane grind of her life.

A familiar face briefly caught Catherine's attention during the journey, triggering memories of childhood chases in a garden with her father. However, the moment of nostalgia dissolved as she realized the man was a stranger, a mere mirage of the past.

Arriving at her office building, she observed a homeless man with a pit bull—a transient scene that momentarily diverted her from the corporate world she was about to reenter.

Her corner office, a haven overlooking the Thames, became the stage for professional intricacies. Grant Mason, a senior figure in the law firm, interrupted her preparations for the meeting with Zane Goldsmith and his formidable father, Zachery.

In the meeting room, Catherine dealt with the details of the case. They talked about whether they should make a deal, what might happen if they went to court, and how to handle the legal plan while also considering how much the firm relies on Goldsmith's business. Zane and Zachery's different personalities made things tense, like setting the stage for a tricky legal fight.

After the meeting, Catherine's phone rang with a call from America. She hesitated before saying no, showing that things from across the ocean were affecting her daily life. The story mixed her work duties with personal uncertainties, and the strange morning with the bad dream and odd encounter continued to hang over her day, making it feel weird.

Catherine's work life, with all its challenges and conflicts, played out against a backdrop of legal stuff, office dynamics, and personal problems. While dealing with the Goldsmith case, her mind, stirred up by the strange morning, created a mix of real life and dreams that was hard to figure out.

In a room with little light, the Goldsmiths were fighting with Catherine about a big legal problem. Zane, the son, was not being friendly and said mean things to Catherine, testing her skills. Then, Zane's dad, Zachery, slapped him hard, making a loud sound.

Despite their apology, the situation remained problematic. Catherine found herself grappling with a challenging case and came up with a notion. Her aim was to portray Zane as a victim of circumstances, highlighting the issues surrounding him that led to his troubles. The room transformed into a battleground of legal discourse as Catherine endeavored to justify the merits of her idea.

But Catherine's phone kept ringing, and it was someone from America. She didn't answer, and this made things feel strange. It hinted that Catherine had two different lives—work and something else—and they were not mixing well.

Later, in her office, Catherine thought a lot about the fight in the meeting. Her boss, Grant, surprised her by saying that maybe Zane should go to prison. This hit Catherine hard because Grant shared a family connection to the situation. His grandson thought Zane was always going to be in trouble. This made the case even more complicated for Catherine.

In the world of laws and family and emotions, Catherine found herself in a story where things weren't clear. The meeting left her with a lot to think about, and Grant's support for Zane going to prison was unexpected. It felt personal because Grant had a family member who knew Zane from school and thought he was always going to cause trouble.

Sitting alone in her office, Catherine faced the challenge of untangling the mess of legal issues and personal connections. The phone call from America, still ringing in her thoughts, added an extra layer of complexity to her day. It was as if there were two worlds—her work world, filled with complex legal problems, and another world, hinted at by the American call, a place where personal matters were pressing in.

As she stared at her desk, the weight of the upcoming trial and the echoes of the phone that kept trying to get her attention made her question the clear lines she thought existed. The room, silent now, held the shadows of difficult decisions and a case that seemed to be stretching beyond the boundaries of the office.

Catherine's journey through this complex narrative continued, with each step bringing her closer to a trial that held not just legal challenges but also personal connections that refused to be ignored. The boundaries between duty and belief, professional and personal, blurred, leaving Catherine to navigate the uncertain path ahead.

In the office, Grant paused, looking serious. He wanted to talk to Catherine, but her phone kept vibrating. She explained it was likely a phishing call from America.

"Let me deal with it," Grant said, taking her phone and answering it sternly. But his tone changed. He handed the phone back to Catherine, saying, "It's for you."

Reluctantly, Catherine answered. On the other end was Sheriff Bob from Teton County, Wyoming. He explained he had some news about her father. The words hit Catherine hard. She was now Ms. Wilson, not Mitchell.

Sheriff Bob's voice delivered the heartbreaking news: her father had passed away. Catherine's hand trembled as the reality sank in. Sensing the news's weight, Grant went to get her some water.

Catherine, shaken, asked how it happened. Sheriff Bob delicately asked when was the last time she saw her father. Her response revealed a painful truth—she hadn't seen him since childhood. The news opened the door to a past she had left behind, bringing with it a flood of emotions and memories. The boundaries between her present life and the echoes of the past seemed to blur in that moment of unexpected loss.

Catherine took a moment to absorb the shock. The news of her father's passing, a man she hadn't seen since childhood, stirred a mixture of emotions—grief, regret, and a cascade of memories she had buried deep within.

Sheriff Bob, empathetic but practical, continued to explain the circumstances of her father's passing. The distance, both in miles and years, seemed to collapse as the sheriff's words painted a picture of a life that had continued in her absence.

CATHERINE(voice shaking): Thank you for letting me know. I... I appreciate it.

BOB: If there's anything you need or if you decide to come here for arrangements, just let us know.

As Catherine ended the call, Grant handed her a glass of water, concern etched on his face.

GRANT: I'm so sorry, Catherine. If you need anything...

Catherine nodded, her mind swirling with memories and unresolved feelings. The weight of the news settled on her like a heavy shroud, and a profound sense of loss enveloped her.

The day, which had begun with the complexities of legal strategies and familial tensions, took an unexpected turn into the realm of personal history. Catherine, now faced with the reality of her father's death, grappled with the emotional aftermath.

In the quiet of her office, with the sounds of the bustling law firm muffled by the closed door, Catherine found herself at a crossroads. The past, long left behind, had resurfaced abruptly, and decisions loomed about how to navigate the path ahead.

As she sat there, the unanswered call from America lingered in her mind, a stark reminder that life's intricacies were as unpredictable as they were complex. Catherine, now grappling with the intersection of personal and professional challenges, faced a journey of self-discovery and reflection that stretched far beyond the confines of her office walls.

In the wake of the startling news, Catherine wrestled with conflicting emotions. Memories, long buried, resurfaced like ghosts from the past. The estrangement from her father, a choice she had made to escape a tumultuous childhood, now stood as an unspoken regret.

GRANT (tentatively): Do you need some time off?

Catherine, still processing the news, shook her head.

CATHERINE: No, I... I need to focus. It's strange; I thought I'd moved on from that part of my life.

GRANT: It's never that easy.

As Grant offered understanding, Catherine focused on the legal complexities that awaited her. The Goldsmith case, once the pinnacle of her concerns, now seemed trivial compared to the intricacies of family ties, strained and unresolved.

Catherine's thoughts flitted back to Wyoming, to a past she had deliberately distanced herself from. She remembered her father as a complicated man, haunted by demons she couldn't comprehend as a child. The news of his death reopened wounds she thought were healed.

Despite the tumult within, Catherine pressed on with her work. The meeting with the Goldsmiths continued, but her mind was divided between legal strategies and memories of a childhood marked by adversity.

Once a tool of intrusion, the phone now served as a conduit to her origins, prompting Catherine to contemplate a pivotal decision: whether to confront a past fraught with painful memories or uphold the meticulously constructed barriers safeguarding her emotions.

Throughout the unfolding day, the conflict between Catherine's personal and professional spheres escalated to a crescendo. The intricate tapestry of her life, woven with legal battles and familial entanglements, took center stage.

In the tranquil interludes between courtroom sessions and phone conversations, Catherine wrestled not only with the complexities of the Goldsmith case but also with the lingering shadows of her own narrative. The journey ahead held the promise of self-discovery and, perhaps, a confrontation with the specters of her past.

Grant suggested they had a drink in his office, so she obliged to this gesture.

In Grant's office, the weight of the news settled heavily on Catherine's shoulders. Grant, understanding the need for a moment of respite, offered a glass of whisky. The smoky windows shielded them from the outside world, creating a private bubble.

"I didn't even know your father was still alive. You never talk about your parents," Grant remarked. A fleeting memory from Catherine's past surfaced—a traumatic departure from her American home, her father's desperate pleas echoing in the background.

"It's not a time of my life I remember much. I came to London when I was 8. I've never been back. My mum didn't..." Catherine trailed off.

"We don't need to talk about it," Grant reassured. The dilemma lingered—Catherine torn between the ghosts of her past and the demands of her present. Sensing her internal struggle, Grant shared a piece of his story.

"Lizzy and I were estranged for the longest time. She never married. Went off to pursue a travel writing career. Got cancer. Died in a tiny village in South America," Grant revealed. Catherine was taken aback.

"It's my biggest regret. But we went over there, after she died. My point is, don't believe your father died like they say he did. You should go and see who he was. You'll regret it otherwise," Grant advised.

"What about my work? The Goldsmith trial?" Catherine questioned.

"It's not until next week. I can oversee the preparation, push for a continuance if necessary," Grant assured, reaching out and taking her hand.

"Go," he urged. Catherine nodded, a mix of apprehension and determination in her gaze. The decision to confront the shadows of her past beckoned, promising not just closure but a journey toward self-discovery.

After leaving the office, Catherine, lost in thought, encounters the homeless man again. He asks for change, and in her emotional turmoil, she gives him a couple of hundred pounds, briefly imagining him as her father.

On the train ride home, Catherine is deep in her thoughts, remembering a happy moment with her father when she was seven.

Later, at home in the kitchen, Catherine, seeking solace, has a glass of wine. The peace is shattered by a car pulling up outside, and Ava, her daughter, rushes in upset. Catherine tries to find out what's wrong, but Ava marches upstairs without answering.

John, Catherine's husband, enters the kitchen, and Catherine questions him about Ava's distress. John reveals that he was trying to share some news with Ava, which led to the emotional scene.

What news?

Vanessa and I are getting married.

Is she pregnant?

What's your reaction?

Well, it's the only reason you married me. So, is she?

That's not the point.

That's entirely the point. How do you think that makes Ava feel?

She's going to be a sister. She's going to have a little brother.

Well, you always wanted a son, so I'm happy for you, John.

Yeah, I can tell.

Catherine, trying to be kind, shifts the conversation.

Sorry. I got some bad news today. My dad died.

Catherine's revelation about her father's death leaves John in disbelief.

"I thought you said he was dead?" John questions, perplexed.

"We didn't know. Mum tried to find him before she passed, but... Anyway, they've asked me to go to Wyoming to sort a few things," Catherine explains.

John reacts with a firm "No."

"I haven't even asked yet," Catherine responds.

"You're her dad," she adds.

"No, I mean I actually can't. I won't be here," John admits.

"Where are you going?" Catherine asks.

John paces, grappling with how to deliver another piece of news. "We... uh, we're moving."

"To where?" Catherine inquires.

"Switzerland. It's where Vanessa's parents are, so they can help when the baby comes. We're flying out this weekend to look for houses. I'll be gone at least a week."

"You have a child. Here. In this country," Catherine points out.

"And we'll figure something out. She can come visit on holidays..." John trails off. The weight of the moment hangs in the air, the news of her father's passing and the impending move to Switzerland creating a web of emotions for Catherine.

"You have a court-mandated custody agreement," Catherine states, frustration evident.

"Ah, the lawyer emerges," John retorts.

"Fine. Just go. Forget all about us and just go!" Catherine exclaims.

"Cathy..." John starts, his sentence truncated as Catherine, consumed by emotions, hurls her wine glass in his direction. He pauses, weighing the prospect of a confrontation, before ultimately deeming it futile. The resounding slam of the door reverberates through the room, and the distant hum of his car gradually dissipates into the nocturnal silence.

Left in solitude, Catherine fixates on the crimson blemish now adorning her kitchen wall. With hesitant steps, she approaches Ava's room, cautiously tapping on the door before cautiously entering.

"Ava, can I come in?" she asks.

Ava lies on her bed, face down on the pillow.

"You're going to anyway," Ava responds.

Catherine sits on the edge of the bed, hesitating to reach out for comfort. She refrains.

"Do you want to talk about the conversation you had with your dad?" Catherine gently inquires.

"It wasn't a conversation. He did all the talking. In order for it to be a conversation, I would have had to have replied, but I didn't," Ava replies, her voice muffled by the pillow. The weight of the news and the complex emotions reverberate through the house.

Catherine's voice carried a gentle tone as she addressed Ava, who lay on her bed, the lingering weight of their conversation palpable in the air.

"Why not?" Catherine inquired softly, seeking to understand.

"He didn't want me to. He doesn't want me. He's starting a new family. I'm nothing to him," Ava responded, her words tinged with a blend of sadness and resignation.

Encouraging Ava to meet her gaze, Catherine watched as Ava slowly turned, her eyes reddened from tears.

"You are not nothing. Your dad is... he's..." Catherine began to say, but Ava interjected.

"He's an arsehole," Ava declared, succinctly encapsulating her emotions.

Catherine accepted the reality with a solemn nod. "Yes, he can be difficult at times, but he's still your dad. You'll still have the opportunity to see him, to maintain a relationship with him. However, let's shift our focus for a moment. I received some news today about my dad. He passed away. Do you understand what that means?"

"He's dead," Ava replied, bluntly acknowledging the harsh truth.

Catherine nodded, her expression grave. "Yes, that's right. And now I need to go on a trip... to bid him farewell, I suppose. I could really use your support during this time. What do you think? Would you like to accompany mommy to America?"

Ava, with a sense of acceptance, replied, "Okay."

"Okay then," Catherine said, and a montage unfolded as they embarked on their journey from London to Wyoming. In the bustling London Heathrow airport, Ava clutched her bright pink backpack.

Catherine settled Ava into her seat on the plane, making sure she had everything she needed for the journey.

As the plane ascended into the sky, Ava gripped the seat tightly, her eyes squeezed shut in trepidation. Catherine, seeking solace in a reassuring touch, felt her daughter's hand adjacent to hers, yet hesitantly unextended. The aircraft surged forward, carrying them towards an unknown horizon.

Upon touchdown at Jackson Hole airport, Ava's countenance blossomed with delight. Excitement radiated from her as she eagerly disembarked from the plane, her eyes alight with wonder at the unfamiliar surroundings. Meanwhile, Catherine's gaze reflected a blend of fatigue and resolve as she focused on the tasks that lay ahead.

Renting a car became the first order of business. While Catherine handled the practicalities, Ava delved into the information about Wyoming on her mother's phone, eager to absorb everything about this unfamiliar place.

On the highway in Wyoming, the rental SUV moved through a landscape vastly different from the one they left behind in London. The forest, the wide spaces, and the towering Teton mountain range created a beautiful contrast to the urban hustle they were accustomed to.

In the rented SUV, Catherine drove while Ava observed the scenery. Ava, always curious, shared a tidbit about the origin of the name "Wyoming." Catherine, surprised and impressed, inquired where Ava had learned this.

Ava, proud of her newfound knowledge, replied, "On the Internet. They mean plain as in land, not plane as in what we just flew on. They didn't have planes back in those days."

Catherine affirmed her correctness with a smile. Ava, not missing a beat, asked, "So you grew up here?" The question hung in the air, inviting a glimpse into Catherine's past.

Catherine, her gaze on the winding road, responded to Ava's question about leaving Wyoming when she was younger.

"Yes. I left when I was just a little younger than you," she admitted. Ava, curious as ever, probed further, "Why did you leave?"

As Catherine pondered how to answer, a vivid flashback gripped her.
FLASHCUT:
Young Catherine sat in the backseat of a car, being driven away from her American home. Her father stood in the far distance, a poignant figure in the middle of the road. Her mother, tears streaming down her face, drove, trying to justify their departure.
CATHERINE'S MOTHER: "It's for the best, Kathy, you hear? It..."
CATHERINE: "...was for the best."
Returning to the present, Ava shifted the conversation to something lighter.
AVA: "Did you ever see a Jackalope?"
CATHERINE: "Jackalopes aren't real, Ava."
AVA: "Are you sure?"
CATHERINE: "Yes, it's just a made-up animal, like the Loch Ness Monster."
AVA, undeterred: "But you can buy a hunting license for Jackalopes."
CATHERINE: "That's just a souvenir for tourists."

AVA, with a mischievous grin: "Well, technically we're tourists, so can we get a license to hunt fake animals?"

Sure enough, hunting was part of the landscape of Catherine's memories. She reluctantly admitted to Ava, "No. No hunting."

As they drove through the outskirts of Jackson, the town exuded old west charm, nestled beneath the imposing Snow King Mountain.

Ava, perched in the passenger seat, soaked in the sights of Main Street. The array of stores, boutiques, and eateries captured her attention. An ice cream parlor, especially, drew her eyes, where children her age savored ice cream cones.

Pulling up at The Antler Inn, a rustic motel, Catherine and Ava stepped out of the SUV. Walking towards the reception, the adventure in Wyoming was unfolding before them.

In the cozy reception of The Antler Inn, Annie, the cheerful receptionist, welcomed Catherine and Ava. The lobby was adorned with a 'hunting lodge' theme, complete with stag heads on the walls and a looming stuffed grizzly in the corner, teeth bared.

AS ANNIE CHECKED THEM in, Catherine inquired about the possibility of extending their stay, depending on how things unfolded. Annie assured her it wouldn't be an issue, given that hunting season was over.

Ava, still curious about the hunting theme, asked about hunting for jackalopes. Annie, with a touch of humor, redirected her attention to more conventional game like mountain lions. Catherine shot Annie a pleading look, silently urging her not to encourage Ava's imagination.

The conversation turned to their origins. Ava proudly declared they were from London, the capital of England, though they lived just outside. Annie, beaming with Wyoming hospitality, expressed delight at having them and assigned them Room 22.

Annie handed Catherine a key with a friendly smile, informing them of a complimentary upgrade due to the low number of guests. Room 22, just a short walk away, became their temporary home at The Antler Inn. Declining help with their bags, Catherine thanked Annie, who assured them of assistance if needed.

In Room 22, the rustic lodge theme continued with wooden interiors. Ava, seemingly lost in thought, gazed out the window at the sun setting behind the mountains, painting the forest in a mystical purple hue. Catherine, trying to engage her daughter, commented on the view.

Ava acknowledged the beauty with a simple "It's pretty." As the day had been long, Catherine proposed a relaxed evening with pizza from a nearby restaurant. With an agreement to keep things simple, mother and daughter settled into their Wyoming retreat, surrounded by the quiet charm of The Antler Inn.

AVA: YES, THAT'S FINE. We normally have pizza on a Friday, but I don't mind if we have it twice in one week

CATHERINE Okay. Let me grab my purse.

AVA And mum?

CATHERINE Yes, rabbit?

AVA, I'm sorry your father passed away and died.

CATHERINE: Thank you for saying that.

Later that night, with empty pizza boxes marking their dinner, Ava is sound asleep. However, Catherine, despite the long day, sits up, grappling with the resurgence of forgotten memories.

In a flashback, young Catherine walks with her father through a forest, sharing smiles on a beautiful day. Joseph, her father, carries a hunting rifle. They later lie on the ground behind a fallen tree, observing a buck in a small clearing. Young Catherine, guided by her father's hands, learns the nuances of handling a gun, a bonding moment in the heart of nature.

Line up your sight just like I showed you. Her father said.

Young Catherine aims at the buck. Her young eyes reflect fear, hesitation, but also adrenaline and excitement.

In the dimly lit room, the faint sound of a gunshot pierced the silence, jolting Catherine awake from her slumber. Confusion clouded her mind as she struggled to make sense of her surroundings. Blinking away the remnants of sleep, Catherine's eyes scanned the unfamiliar room, her heart racing with a sense of urgency.

Panic gripped her chest as she noticed the empty space where Ava's bed should have been. "Ava? Ava?" Catherine's voice echoed in the empty room, met only with silence. Frantically, she searched every corner of the room, her mind racing with fear and uncertainty.

Unable to find any trace of her daughter, Catherine's panic escalated as she dashed out of the room and into the motel car park. The cool night air brushed against her skin as she scanned the area, her eyes darting from one corner to the next in search of any sign of Ava.

Approaching the front desk, Catherine's voice trembled as she addressed Annie, the motel clerk. "Have you seen my daughter?"

Annie's expression softened with sympathy as she responded, "Yes, she was here earlier asking about ice-cream. I told her it was a bit early..."

Desperation clawed at Catherine's heart as she pleaded, "Where did she go?!" Without waiting for a response, she dashed out of the motel and onto Jackson's Main Street, her heart pounding with dread.

Ignoring the curious gazes of the locals, Catherine sprinted towards the ice-cream parlor, her mind racing with a million possibilities. Pushing open the door, she was greeted by the sight of Ava talking to a strange man named Elmer, dressed in a 1950s style diner uniform.

Fury and fear surged through Catherine as she grabbed Ava's arm, her voice trembling with emotion. "What were you thinking?!"

Ava's eyes widened in shock as she started to scream, drawing the attention of the few customers and a junior worker named Dwayne.

Catherine's heart sank as she realized the gravity of the situation, her mind racing with fear and regret.

"Ava, I'm sorry. I'm not touching you. I'm sorry, okay?" Catherine's voice wavered with emotion as she tried to calm her daughter, her heart aching with guilt and worry.

Ava's screams calm into low grunts.

"You can't run off like that. Especially in a strange town."

"It's not that strange."

Catherine acknowledges Elmer.

"Welcome to Elmer's ice-cream parlor. I'm Elmer. And I gather that this is Ava."

"Yes, sorry for the... sorry."

ELMER: Not a problem, not the first child blessed with something special I've had through my door. She was insisting on having breakfast for ice-cream, but I suggested she might like a waffle instead.

DWAYNE: The waffles are really good.

Catherine glances between them in their 1950s uniforms. It is a bit surreal and creepy.

CATHERINE: Sorry, we have a busy day. Come on, Ava.

Ava, realizing she is not getting ice-cream for breakfast, calmly leaves.

ELMER: Come back now, anytime.

Catherine flashes him a phony, polite smile as she leaves.

Ava walks back towards the hotel, Catherine following closely. Unseen by either of them, Ethan (20s) watches from across the street, shadowing them back to the motel. He observes Catherine and Ava get in their SUV and drive off.

They stop in front of the police station. Inside, at the reception area, Catherine and Ava look out of sorts.

Bob appears and immediately spots the pair.

BOB: Ms. Wilson. I'm Sheriff Schaeffer. We spoke on the phone.

He offers his hand, and Catherine shakes it.

Bob led Catherine and Ava to his office, a small space cluttered with files and framed commendations. He gestured for them to sit as he closed the door for privacy.

Catherine, her eyes holding a mix of grief and curiosity, accepted the offer to discuss matters further.

BOB: Your father's over at the county morgue. I can take you over to see him if you like.

CATHERINE: Okay. Do you know... Ava, put these on.

Catherine handed Ava a pair of over-ear headphones and her phone. Bob watched the exchange, curious.

BOB: Do you know how he died?

CATHERINE: The fire department is still looking into the cause of the fire, I'm afraid. I'm hoping to get the report back today.

CATHERINE: You said... he was known...

BOB: I'm going to be straight with you, Ms. Wilson. I've known Joseph Mitchell for fifteen years. He spent many a night in our drunk tank. It got worse after he lost his house. We'd often find him sleeping on the streets, sometimes in the forest. He'd steal from hunters in the season. Truth be told, I found it ironic that you were a lawyer over in London. Like night and day.

Catherine absorbs Bob's revelation, her expression a mix of sadness and recognition of her father's troubled past.

CATHERINE: I had no idea he was living like that. I thought he was... I don't know. He never talked much about his life.

BOB: Addiction can do that to a person. Makes them close off, keep secrets. I'm sorry you're finding out like this.

AVA (through the headphones): Mom, what's happening?

CATHERINE (whispering): Shh, we're talking with the sheriff. I'll fill you in later.

BOB: I can arrange for someone to take you to the morgue when you're ready. Take your time. It's never easy seeing a loved one like that.

CATHERINE: Thank you, Sheriff. We'll go when Ava's ready.

As Bob steps out to make the arrangements, Catherine turns her attention back to Ava.

CATHERINE: Your grandpa faced some tough times, Ava. We'll need to go to the morgue to say our goodbyes.

AVA (removing the headphones): Is he okay?

CATHERINE: No, sweetheart. He's not with us anymore. But we'll handle this together, okay?

AVA: Okay, Mom.

Bob returns, ready to guide them to the morgue. The atmosphere is heavy with the weight of emotions as they navigate the difficult journey of saying farewell to a troubled but complex figure from their past.

Catherine took this in, glancing at Ava, wondering about the connection between her father's troubled past and her daughter's innocence.

CATHERINE: Who do I... How do I make arrangements for his body?

BOB: I can give you the number of a local funeral parlor. They can make any arrangements. We'll need to wait for the fire report to release the body.

CATHERINE: I was hoping to have him cremated.

BOB: They can arrange that, sure. If you're not busy now, I can drive you over to the morgue.

Catherine nodded. They left the office and passed Sheriff Brad Tucker, who was on duty at the reception.

Bob signaled to Brad as they left the police station.

BOB: Brad, I'm just taking Ms. Wilson and her daughter over to the morgue.

BRAD: Do you want the... you know?

BOB: Oh yes, please.

Brad, eager to assist, quickly located an envelope on his desk and handed it to Bob, who then passed it to Catherine.

BOB: These were some of your father's effects that we recovered.

CATHERINE: Thank you.

Inside Bob's police car, Catherine and Ava sat in the back while Bob drove.

AVA: Your car smells of dog.

BOB: That's because I have a partner who is a canine.

AVA: Where is he?

BOB: She. Her name's Callie. She's in her kennel, just now resting.

Catherine opened the envelope, revealing a wedding ring, a necklace with a St. Christopher pendant, some old coins, and a charred Polaroid photo of Joseph and a younger Catherine. A tear escaped Catherine's eye. She wiped it away and carefully put the contents back in the envelope.

The police car pulled up at the county morgue. Bob led Catherine and Ava through the somber halls, the air thick with the sterile scent of disinfectant and the weight of the unavoidable.

After Catherine had viewed the charred remains of her father in the morgue, she stepped back into the stark corridor.

BOB: You go in. I'll stay here with Ava.

CATHERINE: Be good for the sheriff, Ava.

Catherine entered the morgue, where a lanky coroner named Elias awaited. Elias, in his 50s, greeted Catherine with an unsettling smile.

ELIAS: I'm sorry for your loss. Please, prepare yourself. The body has suffered severe burns and tissue loss.

Catherine nodded silently. Elias uncovered the body, revealing the aftermath of the fire. The memory of her father standing proudly over a dead buck flashed in her mind before reality snapped back.

ELIAS: I'll give you a moment.

As Catherine grieved privately, Ava chatted with Bob in the hallway.

AVA: Sheriff, does my grandpa go to heaven now?

BOB: Well, Ava, that's something people believe in different ways. Some say yes, some aren't sure. What do you think?

AVA: I hope he does. He was nice.

BOB: I'm sure he was. Heaven's got room for nice people.

Ava nodded, processing the idea of heaven in her innocent way.

Meanwhile, Elias discreetly handed Catherine a small urn and explained the process of arranging the cremation. Catherine, still grappling with the reality of her father's death, thanked Elias and rejoined Ava and Bob in the hallway.

CATHERINE: We can go now.

BOB: You okay?

CATHERINE: As okay as I can be, I suppose.

Bob led them back to the police car, where Callie eagerly awaited, her tail wagging as they approached.

BOB: I'll take you back to the station. You can arrange the cremation from there.

Catherine nodded, appreciating the sheriff's assistance during this challenging time.

Back at the police station, Catherine made the necessary calls to arrange the cremation while Ava occupied herself with drawing pictures in the corner. The atmosphere was somber, yet Bob's presence provided a comforting anchor.

CATHERINE: Thank you, Sheriff Schaffer.

BOB: Please, call me Bob.

"Okay, Bob," Catherine acknowledged as they left the police station. Bob went back inside, tending to his duties.

Bob took off in his car, promising to check in the next day. As they entered their room, Catherine couldn't help but feel a mixture of exhaustion and gratitude for Bob's support.

CATHERINE, EAGER TO mend the rift between herself and Ava, suggested a visit to the Elk Sanctuary after spotting an advertisement in town. Despite Ava's lingering grudge, she reluctantly agreed to the outing.

As they embarked on their journey, the SUV climbed a winding highway, navigating through a picturesque valley adorned with towering trees. Following the signs for the Elk Sanctuary, they turned onto a narrower road, delving deeper into the wilderness.

Unbeknownst to them, Ethan watched from his car across the road, his gaze fixed on Catherine and Ava as they returned to their vehicle. Deciding to tail them discreetly, Ethan kept a safe distance as they continued their drive.

Inside the SUV, Catherine attempted to bridge the gap with Ava, who still harbored some resentment from the ice cream incident. Their conversation was interrupted by a flashing warning light on the dashboard, signaling a potential issue with the vehicle.

"Mom, can we have ice cream for dinner?" Ava asked hopefully, her voice tinged with a hint of mischief.

Catherine smiled, knowing that a warm meal would be more suitable given the chilly weather. "Sweetheart, I think we need something warm tonight. How about we find a nice place for dinner?" she suggested, hoping to indulge Ava's sweet tooth without derailing their plans.

"Okay, as long as they have dessert," Ava replied with a grin, striking a playful deal with her mother as they continued their journey towards the Elk Sanctuary.

The rain drummed relentlessly against the forest canopy as Catherine and Ava hurried through the dense foliage, their footsteps muffled by the damp earth beneath their feet. The ominous gray clouds overhead cast a shadow over the secluded stretch of road, enveloping the surrounding woods in an eerie silence broken only by the patter of raindrops.

Catherine's heart sank as she surveyed their surroundings, her brow furrowing in concern as she realized they were completely cut off from the outside world. "Oh, darn," she muttered under her breath, her voice barely audible over the sound of the rain. Glancing down at Ava, she offered a reassuring smile, her attempt to mask her growing unease.

"Don't pay attention to that," she whispered to Ava, her voice tinged with forced optimism as she sought to shield her daughter from the mounting tension. Turning her attention back to their predicament, Catherine scanned the area for any sign of help, her eyes settling on a payphone mounted on the wall of a nearby building.

"Hello?" she called out tentatively, her voice echoing in the empty silence. When no response came, she approached the payphone and lifted the receiver, only to be met with static on the line. Frustration etched across her features as she glanced down at her phone, confirming what she already feared – no signal.

"This isn't good," Catherine murmured to herself, her voice laced with concern as she realized the gravity of their situation. Ava, sensing her mother's unease, offered a word of comfort. "I don't like it either. Let's head back to the car," she suggested, her voice tinged with apprehension.

Nodding in agreement, Catherine led Ava back through the rain-soaked forest, their pace quickening as they sought refuge in the shelter of their rented SUV. As they approached the vehicle, Catherine noticed another car parked nearby, a solitary figure standing beside it. It was Ethan.

"Hey there," Ethan called out, his voice cutting through the silence like a beacon of hope. "I noticed you stopped. Wondered if you needed help." Catherine hesitated for a moment, her mind racing as she weighed her options. "No, thanks. We're good," she replied, her tone polite but firm as she declined his offer of assistance. "We called the rental company, and they're sending someone to help us."

Ethan's expression darkened as he shook his head, a knowing smile playing at the corners of his lips. "Well, that won't work, Catherine," he remarked cryptically. "No signal out here in the wild greenwoods." Catherine's heart sank as she realized the extent of their isolation, a sense of dread settling over her like a heavy cloak.

Catherine and Ava, now back at the SUV, exchanged worried glances. The forest seemed to loom around them, the rain continuing its relentless assault on the dense canopy above. Ethan's words had cast a shadow of doubt over their plans, leaving them feeling vulnerable and uncertain about their next move.

"I live around here. If you don't mind waiting, I can give you a lift to the nearest town," Ethan offered, his voice tinged with a hint of concern. Catherine hesitated, her gaze flickering between Ethan and the safety of their car. "That's kind of you, but we're expecting someone from the rental company," she replied, her tone cautious.

Ethan shrugged nonchalantly, a knowing smile playing at the corners of his lips. "Suit yourself. But don't count on that signal coming back anytime soon. These woods have a way of swallowing up the signals," he warned cryptically as he retreated to his car.

Catherine wrestled with conflicting emotions, torn between heeding a local's advice and sticking to their original plan. Ava, sensing her mother's indecision, looked up with questioning eyes, silently seeking reassurance.

"Let's give it a little more time. The rental company might send someone, and I'd rather not take a ride with a stranger in the middle of nowhere," Catherine decided, her voice tinged with uncertainty. Ava nodded in agreement, her expression mirroring her mother's concerns.

They settled into the car, the rhythmic patter of rain on the roof creating a sense of isolation. Minutes stretched into eternity as Catherine periodically checked her phone for a signal that remained stubbornly elusive.

"We can't just sit here indefinitely. I'll try calling the rental company again," Catherine announced, her frustration evident in her voice. Despite her efforts, the phone remained stubbornly unresponsive, adding to their growing sense of unease.

"What if we run out of gas waiting here?" Ava voiced her concern, her tone laced with worry. Catherine forced a reassuring smile, trying to alleviate Ava's fears. "We'll cross that bridge when we come to it. Let's hope someone shows up soon," she replied, her own anxiety simmering beneath the surface.

The confines of the SUV became a refuge from the persistent rain, but the tension inside grew with each passing moment. Catherine contemplated their limited options, feeling the weight of responsibility for Ava's safety pressing down on her shoulders.

As if on cue, Ethan approached the SUV again, his expression sympathetic. "Still no luck with that phone, huh?" he remarked, his tone filled with understanding. Catherine nodded, a sense of gratitude mingling with her cautiousness. "Unfortunately not. We'll just have to be patient," she replied, her voice tinged with resignation.

"Look, I get it. These woods can be tricky. If you change your mind, my offer stands. I can take you to town and maybe help you figure things out," Ethan offered, his sincerity evident in his tone. Catherine thanked him, her gratitude tempered by a lingering sense of caution. "Thank you. We'll wait a little longer," she replied, her voice filled with uncertainty.

"Well, that won't work, Catherine. No signal out here in the wild greenwoods," Ethan reiterated, his words echoing in the confines of the car as he retreated once more into the rain-soaked forest.

Worried about Ava's safety, Catherine stands in front of her daughter like a lioness guarding her cub, her heart pounding with fear and determination. The gas station's fluorescent lights cast eerie shadows around them as they stand in the dimly lit corridor, surrounded by an unsettling silence broken only by the distant hum of machinery.

"Hello?" Catherine calls out, her voice echoing through the empty space. There's no response except for the faint rustle of leaves outside, carried in by the chilly night breeze. Her eyes dart around the deserted area, searching for any sign of help or hope.

Spotting a payphone on the wall, Catherine's mind races with possibilities. She strides over to it and picks up the receiver, her fingers trembling with anticipation. But her hopes are dashed as she hears nothing but static on the line. Desperation claws at her as she checks her phone again, praying for a signal that refuses to appear.

Suddenly, a voice cuts through the silence, sending shivers down Catherine's spine. "Names don't matter. What matters is, you've come back to us. We were hoping you might. And you brought us a gift. A special gift," the voice says, its tone dripping with sinister intent. Catherine's blood runs cold as she realizes Ethan is addressing her, his words laden with ominous implications.

With a surge of urgency, Catherine turns to Ava, her voice trembling with fear as she gives her daughter instructions. "Run back to the gas station and hide when I say so," she urges, her eyes pleading with Ava to understand the gravity of the situation. But before Ava can move, chaos erupts around them.

Two masked men materialize from the shadows, their presence sending a jolt of terror coursing through Catherine's veins. She barely has time to react before one of them lunges forward, striking her with a brutal blow that sends her crashing to the ground, pain shooting through her body like a lightning bolt.

Ava's screams pierce the air as the other masked man seizes her, his hands closing around her small frame with a vice-like grip. Catherine's heart lurches with agony as she watches helplessly, her vision blurring with tears of anguish and despair.

In a flash, the masked man presses a cloth soaked in chloroform against Ava's face, her cries fading into unconsciousness as darkness envelops her. Catherine's world spins out of control as she struggles to make sense of the nightmare unfolding before her eyes, her every instinct screaming for her to fight back, to protect her daughter at all costs.

It all happens so fast. The sudden appearance of Ethan, the cryptic talk, and then the abrupt violence that separates Catherine from Ava. The rain outside mirrors the turmoil inside Catherine as fear and confusion grip her. She struggles to comprehend the events, her mind racing to make sense of the danger that has befallen them in the heart of the wild greenwoods.

The situation escalates from an unexpected encounter to a desperate struggle for safety. Catherine, now alone and disoriented, fights against the shock and pain, her thoughts consumed by the need to find Ava and escape the looming threat that lurks in the shadows of the mysterious woods.

As Catherine grapples with the unfolding nightmare, the world around her becomes a blur of rain-soaked fear and desperate determination. The gas station, once a brief refuge, transforms into a battleground of emotions, with echoes of Ava's scream haunting Catherine's every step. The story takes a dark turn, plunging deeper into uncertainty and suspense, leaving Catherine to navigate the treacherous path ahead in pursuit of her daughter and the answers that elude her grasp.

Catherine, all beaten up, tries to get to Ava but gets hit again. She falls onto the road and sees her daughter being taken away into the forest. Even though she's hurt, Catherine stands up, determined, and tries to follow the vehicle. But it disappears with Ava.

Left alone, soaked in the rain, Catherine stands there, shocked and uncertain about what to do next. Eventually, she decides to run back to the SUV.

Inside the rented car, Catherine repeatedly tries to start it, but it refuses to cooperate. Frustration takes over, and she screams while hitting the steering wheel in desperation.

Undeterred, Catherine dashes back toward the main highway, clutching her phone tightly, hopeful for a signal. As she reaches the highway, a single bar appears on her phone screen, a small glimmer of hope amid the relentless rain.

In Bob's police car, Catherine tells the sheriff everything that happened. She explains how their car stopped, they tried to get help, and when they came back, a man who knew them showed up. Then two others came, and they took Ava.

Bob, understanding how serious it is, tells Catherine to show him where it happened. Catherine notices Callie, the German Shepherd, in the back seat. When they get to her SUV, Bob checks everything out and grabs Ava's pink backpack.

Back in the police car, Bob gives the backpack to Catherine and asks her which way the abductors went. Catherine, shaking from the cold, points away from the highway. Bob tries to contact Brad, the sheriff on duty, but all they get is static.

Unfazed by the challenges ahead, Bob decides to prioritize Catherine's safety and take her back to town. As they drive, he plans to issue an Amber alert for Ava, holding onto the hope of bringing her back home.

Slowly regaining awareness, Catherine opens her eyes to find her colleague, Bob, standing nearby. The car, now a charred wreck, emits smoke nearby. Bob rushes to extinguish the remaining flames before peering inside the vehicle.

"It's empty," he informs her, his voice carrying a mixture of relief and concern.

Catherine, still shaky, begins to feel a surge of panic. Sensing her distress, Bob encourages her to take deep breaths, guiding her until her racing heart begins to calm down.

As the rain intensifies, Bob surveys the area, his gaze landing on a nearby hiking trail. With determination, he turns to Catherine. "I'm going to take Callie and search the forest. You stay in the patrol car."

However, Catherine refuses to be sidelined. "No," she insists, her voice trembling but resolute. "I can't just sit here. Let me come with you. We can split up and cover more ground."

Bob hesitates, considering the potential dangers of navigating through the dense forest. "It's dangerous," he cautions, locking eyes with Catherine. "If you get lost..."

Catherine meets his gaze with determination. "I'll be careful," she promises, displaying resolve despite the uncertainty that lies ahead.

Concern etched on her face, Catherine confronts Bob amidst the aftermath of the car fire.

"There's something you're not telling me," she asserts urgently.

Bob hesitates for a moment, then confesses, "I found a pink backpack in the car. Is it Ava's?"

A wave of fear tightens Catherine's heart as she grasps the gravity of the situation. "What's happening that you're not telling me?" she inquires, her voice trembling.

Bob looks directly at her. "Ms. Wilson, does the backpack belong to your daughter?"

Catherine's breath catches in her throat as she acknowledges, "Yes."

Without further explanation, Bob retrieves the backpack from the car and presents it to Callie, the loyal German Shepherd at his side. Callie sniffs the bag diligently, her trained senses poised for any potential clue.

""Okay, girl. Let's take a good look at this, huh?" Bob encourages, unzipping the backpack and revealing its contents to Callie.

While Callie diligently investigates, Bob prepares for the next steps. He grabs his own daypack, slinging it over his shoulders along with a rifle.

"Let's head into the woods," he decides, his tone resolute. "The trees will protect us from the rain, and hopefully, Callie can catch a scent."

With unwavering determination, Bob leads the way into the dense forest, Callie bounding ahead with her nose to the ground. Catherine hesitates for a moment, torn between the safety of the police car and the urgent need to find her daughter. She takes a deep breath and follows Bob and Callie into the unknown terrain, her heart heavy with both fear and hope.

As Catherine watches Bob and Callie navigate the dense forest, her heart races with anticipation, their mission to find Ava hanging in the balance.

"Does she have something?" Catherine asks nervously, her eyes switching between Bob and the determined canine.

"Not yet," Bob answers, his voice steady despite the urgency of their search.

"How big are these forests?" Catherine questions, her voice tinged with worry.

"Big. Real big," Bob responds simply. "But we don't need to cover the whole forest. Just the part she went. That's why we got Callie."

They forge ahead along a winding path, sheltered from the rain by the canopy of branches overhead. Suddenly, Callie pauses, her senses alert to a scent only she can detect. With a sharp bark, she signals to Bob before darting off into the underbrush.

"Now she's got something," Bob declares, urgency lacing his words. "Stay close."

Catherine struggles to keep pace, her feet stumbling over uneven terrain. With a determined effort, she pushes forward, only to trip and fall to the ground. Dusting herself off, she calls out desperately into the wilderness, "Bob? Sheriff Schaeffer? Hello?"

In the distance, Bob's voice carries through the trees, cutting through the silence like a lifeline. "We got something!"

With renewed determination, Catherine picks herself up and jogs to meet him, her heart pounding with hope and fear intertwined.

Amidst the dense trees and steep slopes of the forest, Bob and Catherine stand together, their eyes scanning the rugged terrain for any sign of Ava.

Catherine's heart pounds as she navigates the slope, her footing unsure until Bob steadies her with a firm grip. In that fleeting moment of closeness, a sense of trust and connection passes between them.

"It's okay. I gotcha," Bob reassures her, ensuring she's stable before releasing his hold. Catherine's gaze falls upon Callie, the faithful companion sitting nearby, her attention drawn to a bush adorned with distinct blue threads.

"When I saw her this morning, Ava was wearing a blue woolen sweater," Bob remarks, a glimmer of hope in his eyes as he points out the threads.

Catherine's smile mirrors his optimism. "We're on the right track," she declares with determination.

But Bob's expression darkens, a shadow of doubt crossing his features. "The men who took Ava," he begins, his voice laced with concern. "They might be trying to throw us off the trail."

Catherine's resolve wavers as she considers the possibility. "Or she might have fallen and tried to run away," she counters, her voice tinged with uncertainty. "You can't second-guess everything."

""I'm not second-guessing," Bob insists, his tone firm. "But if we head in the wrong direction, it could cost us precious time."

Catherine furrows her brow, pondering Bob's words. "Why do you think they would have left these for us to find?" she questions, her mind racing with possibilities as they continue their search, the mystery of Ava's disappearance unfolding amidst the rugged beauty of the forest.

Bob's revelation hangs heavy in the air as Catherine processes the chilling truth. "Ava isn't the first girl to go missing around here," Bob admits, his voice weighted with solemnity.

Catherine's breath catches in her throat. "What? How many?" she demands, her voice trembling with disbelief.

"Ten in the last years," Bob reveals, his words landing like a heavy blow. "And that's just the ones that got reported. All around Ava's age."

"Why didn't you warn us? We're tourists here?!" Catherine's voice rises with a mixture of shock and anger, her accusatory gaze fixed on Bob.

"I didn't want to scare you unnecessarily," Bob explains, his tone tinged with regret. "You had enough on your plate."

Catherine's frustration boils over as she lashes out, her words sharp with accusation. "I think you didn't want to tell a lawyer how bad you are at your job!"

Bob's expression softens, a flicker of understanding in his eyes. "You're upset, I understand," he acknowledges. "I just... I want to be honest with you about what I think is happening. The other missing girls..."

"Ava isn't missing. She was taken!" Catherine interjects, her voice resolute as she points towards the bush adorned with threads. "And we're wasting time. I say we go this way."

Bob nods, his gaze scanning the ground for any trace of evidence. Together, they set off into the forest, their determination to find Ava driving them forward amidst the haunting echoes of past disappearances.

As the search intensifies, Bob leads Callie to the bush adorned with blue threads, urging the loyal canine to sniff for any trace of a scent. Callie sniffs around the ground before picking up a scent in a different direction, prompting her to give chase.

"If you want to go that way, on you go, but Callie says it's this way. She's never wrong," Bob insists, his trust in the canine unwavering.

Catherine, fueled by determination and desperation, follows Callie's lead, her eyes fixed on the forest ahead.

As they venture deeper into the forest, the trees thickening around them, the rain eases but is replaced by a squalling breeze that sends shivers down Catherine's spine. Bob notices her discomfort and offers an explanation.

"We call it a howling wind," he explains, his voice tinged with empathy.

Catherine's attention shifts as she realizes Callie has disappeared from sight. Bob whistles a few times, and the faithful dog reappears from the deep undergrowth.

"Go Callie. Go!" Bob encourages, urging the dog to continue leading the way. With Callie once again forging ahead, the trio continues their determined pursuit.

Amidst the tense silence of the forest, Catherine's curiosity breaks through the air of urgency. "Did you ever get any of the girls back?" she asks, her voice barely above a whisper.

Bob's expression darkens as he shakes his head, the weight of past failures heavy on his shoulders, their grim reality looming over the unfolding search for Ava.

As Bob and Catherine press on through the dense forest, their conversation turns to the grim reality of past search efforts. "Had different sheriff departments, even the FBI on one of them, but nothing," Bob admits, his voice tinged with frustration.

"Catherine, however, was not willing to be left behind. The urgency to find Ava outweighed any fear she had of the turbulent river. "No, I'm going with you," she declared, her voice determined despite the knot of anxiety in her stomach.

With a nod, Bob began carefully navigating the slippery stones, choosing each step with precision. Callie followed, demonstrating a grace that belied her canine nature. The river roared below them, its intimidating force evident with each passing moment.

Catherine took a deep breath, suppressing the fear that threatened to take hold. Placing her trust in Bob's lead, she cautiously stepped onto the first stone, her eyes locked on the distant shore. The stones were uneven and slick with rain, making every step a calculated risk.

The trio moved in unison, a careful dance across the stepping stones. Callie's paws, accustomed to various terrains, found secure footholds, while Bob maintained a steady pace, offering a helping hand when needed.

As they reached the midpoint of the river, the current beneath grew stronger, and the stones more challenging to navigate. Catherine's heart raced, the adrenaline coursing through her veins. She stumbled but regained her balance with Bob's support.

The daunting challenge forced them into a focused silence, broken only by the rush of the river. Callie's keen senses remained alert, contributing to the unspoken understanding between them – every step forward was a step toward finding Ava.

Upon reaching the opposite bank, a collective sigh of relief escaped them. The forest on this side seemed denser, the shadows thicker, but the trio pressed on. The urgency to find Ava propelled them forward, following the faint trail that led deeper into the woods.

As they ventured into the heart of the forest, the undergrowth became denser, and the terrain more challenging. Bob led the way with an unwavering determination, Callie at his side. Catherine, despite the physical exertion, matched their pace, her determination fueled by the love for her missing daughter.

The woods seemed to close in around them, the tangled branches forming a natural barrier. A sense of isolation permeated the air, intensifying the gravity of their search. Every rustle of leaves and snapping twig heightened their senses, amplifying the tension that hung in the forest.

"Bob, do you have any idea where they might have taken Ava?" Catherine asked, breaking the silence as they navigated through the labyrinth of trees.

Bob's expression tightened, his brows furrowed with concentration. "There's an old cabin not too far from here. Some folks say it's abandoned, but I've seen signs of recent activity. It's worth checking."

The mention of a cabin heightened Catherine's apprehension, but her determination remained unyielding. "Let's go there. We need to find Ava," she urged, her voice resolute.

The forest path led them towards the rumored cabin, hidden within the shadows of the ancient trees. The air grew thick with suspense as they approached, the distant echoes of their footsteps accompanying the rhythmic chorus of nature.

Upon reaching the clearing that housed the cabin, Bob motioned for them to stay behind while he and Callie approached cautiously. The cabin stood weathered, its wooden facade showing signs of neglect. Yet, there was an undeniable aura of recent activity – a hint of smoke wafted from the chimney.

Catherine's heart pounded as she awaited Bob's signal. Callie's alert stance hinted at a potential presence within. Bob signaled for them to join him, and they cautiously entered the cabin, the creaking door echoing through the silence.

Inside, the cabin revealed signs of a hasty departure – a flickering lantern, an overturned chair. The remnants of a struggle were evident. In a corner, Catherine spotted a piece of Ava's torn sweater, confirming her worst fears.

"We're on the right track," Bob whispered, his eyes scanning the room.

Determined and fueled by a surge of adrenaline, the trio pressed on. Their search for Ava had taken a dark turn, but the glimmer of hope burned brighter as they followed the trail within the heart of the enigmatic forest.

With the immediate danger subsided, Catherine's shivering body slowly regained warmth beneath the blanket. Bob's eyes held a mixture of concern and relief as he observed her, still processing the intensity of the river crossing.

"Thank you," Catherine whispered, her voice barely audible above the lingering echoes of the rushing water. Bob nodded, the unspoken acknowledgment of their shared ordeal passing between them.

As they regrouped on the riverbank, a renewed determination fueled their collective resolve. The trail that lay ahead promised answers, and they pressed on, guided by the unwavering loyalty of Callie, who had been a steadfast companion through the challenges they faced.

The forest enveloped them once more, its ancient trees casting elongated shadows as the moonlight filtered through the dense canopy. Bob led the way, his senses attuned to the surroundings, and Callie trailed close behind, her nose to the ground.

Their journey through the woods was marked by an unspoken understanding—a shared purpose that bound them together. The mystery of Ava's disappearance became intertwined with their own quest for survival and resilience in the face of adversity.

As they walked, the quietude of the forest was broken by a distant howl. Bob's expression tightened, a hint of concern etching lines across his forehead. "That's a wolf," he remarked, glancing at Catherine. "Don't worry, they usually keep their distance."

Catherine's eyes widened with a mixture of fear and curiosity. The haunting call echoed through the trees, creating an eerie ambiance that added another layer of complexity to their journey. Despite the uncertainty, they pressed on, determined to uncover the truth hidden within the heart of the forest.

As the terrain varied, with uneven ground and fallen branches underfoot, Catherine struggled to keep up with Bob's steady pace. The adrenaline from the river incident waned, replaced by a persistent fatigue that gnawed at her limbs.

"Take your time," Bob encouraged, casting a glance over his shoulder. "We're not in a hurry. We just need to keep moving."

Catherine nodded gratefully, her appreciation for Bob's understanding evident. The forest seemed to stretch endlessly before them, a maze of shadows and secrets. Yet, their journey carried a purpose that transcended the challenges of the wilderness.

Amidst the dense foliage, a clearing emerged, revealing a natural amphitheater bathed in moonlight. The forest's breath seemed to pause as they entered this open space, a sanctuary within the ancient grove. It was a momentary respite, a chance to catch their breath and reflect on the journey thus far.

Catherine's gaze drifted to the starlit sky, a canvas painted with countless constellations. She couldn't help but wonder if Ava was somewhere beneath the same celestial tapestry, watching over them. The thought fueled her determination, infusing renewed energy into her weary limbs.

Bob broke the silence, his voice carrying a sense of purpose. "We're getting close to that cabin. Just a little farther." The mention of the cabin reignited Catherine's focus as they ventured deeper into the heart of the forest.

The trees gradually gave way to a small clearing, and there it stood—the rumored cabin, a silent witness to the secrets hidden within the woods. Bob motioned for silence as they approached, their cautious steps ensuring the element of surprise.

Callie, sensing the shift in atmosphere, moved ahead with stealth, her trained instincts alert to any potential danger. The cabin's weathered facade hinted at years of abandonment, yet the signs of recent activity were unmistakable.

Bob signaled for Catherine to stay back as he approached the cabin door. A low creak echoed through the night as he pushed it open, revealing a dimly lit interior. The air was thick with anticipation as they crossed the threshold into the unknown.

The flickering flame of an oil lamp revealed a scene frozen in time—an overturned chair, scattered papers, and remnants of a struggle. Catherine's breath caught as she noticed a torn piece of Ava's sweater, a tangible link that connected them to the enigma surrounding the cabin.

Bob's eyes scanned the room, a mix of concern and determination etched across his face. "They were here," he murmured, the gravity of the situation settling in.

The journey through the forest had brought them to this pivotal moment—the heart of the mystery that shrouded Ava's disappearance. Their quest for answers intensified within the confines of the cabin, the echoes of a struggle urging them to unravel the truth concealed within the shadows.

Jared, struggling to breathe, finally speaks, "We were heading to the old mine. The one on Pine Ridge." His words hang in the air, and Bob's stern expression deepens.

Under the relentless onslaught of rain, Bob's expression remained steely as he confronted Jared, his voice laced with a palpable threat. "You better start making real sense real quick now, or I will leave you here to bleed out," he growled, his eyes narrowed in suspicion. Jared's gaze flickered towards Catherine, a silent acknowledgment passing between them, but she feigned ignorance, her voice trembling with uncertainty. "I don't know what he's talking about," she insisted, her words a desperate plea for Bob's trust.

Despite his skepticism, Bob had no reason to doubt Catherine's sincerity. With a heavy sigh, he shifted his attention to their immediate predicament as rain continued to pour down upon them. "There's an old hunter's cabin not far from here. We'll take him there, get you warm," he declared, his tone firm and decisive. "You try anything, I'll shoot your other leg," he warned Jared, his gaze unwavering as he made it clear he wouldn't hesitate to act if necessary.

With grim determination, Bob and Catherine hoisted Jared up and began to drag him deeper into the forest, their footsteps muffled by the sound of raindrops pounding against the forest floor. Through the dense foliage, an old cabin emerged, its weathered facade a testament to years of neglect and decay. Callie, their faithful companion, led the way, her keen senses alert to any potential danger as she cautiously approached the cabin.

Bob surveyed the dilapidated structure with a critical eye, noting its precarious condition before gesturing for Catherine to proceed inside with Jared. "No one's home. Let's go," he remarked tersely, his grip on his rifle tightening as he prepared to enter the cabin. With a nod of understanding, Catherine dragged Jared across the threshold, her heart pounding with a mixture of fear and determination as she braced herself for whatever lay ahead.

As Bob worked swiftly to ignite a fire in the decrepit cabin, Catherine watched anxiously, her concern evident in her furrowed brow. "Won't they see the smoke?" she voiced her worry, casting a wary glance at the billowing clouds of gray that rose from the fireplace. Bob paused momentarily, his rugged features softened by a reassuring smile. "Probably not in this rain. Stand here and get warm," he instructed Catherine, his tone gentle yet firm as he ushered her closer to the crackling flames.

Meanwhile, Jared's desperate attempts to escape were thwarted by Bob's relentless grip, his struggles futile against the hunter's superior strength. With a swift motion, Bob hurled Jared to the dusty floor, his foot pressing down on the intruder's throat with unwavering resolve. "No more bullshit. I'm going to take my foot away, and you better start singing like a gospel choir or you are going to see a whole new side to your friendly sheriff," Bob's voice echoed through the cabin, his words a menacing promise as he brandished his gun with chilling authority.

Jared nodded frantically, the pressure on his throat relenting as he gasped for air. "What are you doing out here?" Bob demanded, his steely gaze locked onto Jared's trembling form. Jared's voice quivered as he spoke, his words laden with fear and desperation. "We come to pay tribute... to the forest. There are forces deep in these trees. Ancient forces. They demand tribute," he confessed, his eyes darting nervously around the dimly lit cabin.

Bob's brow furrowed in disbelief, his mind racing to comprehend the gravity of Jared's revelation. The forest, once a place of solace and sanctuary, now loomed ominously with untold secrets and ancient powers. As the fire crackled in the hearth, casting dancing shadows upon the worn walls of the cabin, Bob and Catherine exchanged a knowing glance, their resolve strengthened by the realization that they were entangled in a struggle far greater than they could have ever imagined.

In the dimly lit cabin, the tension hung heavy in the air as Jared's ominous words reverberated through the room. Catherine's heart pounded in her chest, her mind reeling with disbelief at the sinister revelation unfolding before her. "You mean..." Bob's voice trailed off, his features contorted with a mixture of shock and anger as he struggled to comprehend Jared's chilling confession.

Jared nodded solemnly, his gaze unwavering as he confirmed Bob's worst fears. "Yes," he uttered, his voice a haunting whisper that sent shivers down Catherine's spine. Catherine's eyes widened in horror, her hands trembling as she grappled with the weight of Jared's words. "What do you mean? What does he mean?" she implored, her voice trembling with fear and confusion.

Jared's lips curled into a sinister smile as he elaborated on the sinister truth that had been concealed in the shadows of the forest for far too long. "Your girl... she's our tribute. It was going to be you. The tribute has to be young, see, innocent. But we were going to make an exception for you. The one that got away," he explained, his words dripping with malice as he revealed the twisted machinations of their dark ritual.

Catherine staggered back, her mind reeling with disbelief at the horrifying revelation. Images flashed through her mind, memories of her childhood spent running through the forest, the gentle glow of fireflies illuminating the night as she reveled in the innocence of youth. "I don't know," she whispered, her voice barely above a hoarse murmur as she struggled to process the magnitude of Jared's revelation.

Bob's jaw clenched with fury, his eyes ablaze with righteous anger as he turned his attention back to Jared. "You killed her father," he accused, his voice laced with raw emotion as he confronted the sinister figure before him. Jared's smirk widened into a malevolent grin as he shrugged off Bob's accusation with callous indifference. "Not me," he retorted, his tone dripping with disdain as he brazenly denied his involvement in the heinous crime.

"But someone in your sick little club," Bob pressed on, his voice laced with contempt as he confronted Jared with the truth. Jared's leer deepened, his eyes glinting with malicious intent as he reveled in Bob's righteous indignation. "Like you said, I own a fishing shop. I know how to bait a big fish," he taunted, his words a chilling reminder of the darkness that lurked beneath the surface of their seemingly idyllic surroundings.

Turning to Catherine, he offers solace amid the chaos. "You scumbag! How could you do that to a little girl!?" Catherine screams, her rage unleashed as she pounds on Jared.

Bob intervenes, pulling Catherine away, wrestling with her grief and anger. Jared, on the ground, writhes in pain. "Their tribute keeps the spirits at bay. Without it, this world would be plunged into darkness," Jared claims, desperation tainting his voice.

Bob dismisses Jared's words, firm in his skepticism. "Don't listen to him; he's out of his mind," he declares, his eyes revealing the inner turmoil.

Jared's confession ignites a fire within Bob, who erupts in a fury. He mercilessly beats Jared with the butt of his rifle until blood stains the floor beneath the broken man.

Catherine, faced with the gruesome aftermath, accuses Bob in a trembling voice, "You killed him! He knew where Ava was, and you killed him!" Bob, his demeanor softened, stammers with remorse, "One of the girls... she was my... And I... I'm sorry."

Before they can grapple with the weight of this revelation, gunfire shatters the fragile calm. Callie yelps in pain as a bullet grazes her, and Bob and Catherine instinctively drop to the floor, seeking refuge from the onslaught.

"When the shooting stops, I'm going to run out and draw their fire. You run in the opposite direction," Bob instructs Catherine, urgency coloring his voice. He hands her a handgun, preparing for a calculated risk in their desperate bid for survival.

As the chaos subsides, Bob dashes out of the cabin, luring the attackers' fire away from Catherine. She cautiously peers through the doorway, witnessing a masked figure standing over Jared's lifeless body.

The masked man removes his disguise, revealing himself as Ethan—the same young man who abducted Ava. Catherine tightens her grip on the gun, stepping forward with a mix of fear and determination.

"Where is my daughter?" Catherine demands, her voice trembling with urgency. Unfazed, Ethan calmly assures her, "She's safe. I can take you to her."

Catherine hesitates, her uncertainty palpable. Yet, Ethan's ominous words send shivers down her spine. "Not far. I just need you to do something for me first," he taunts, a sinister smile playing on his lips.

Before Catherine can react, Ethan lunges for her gun, wrestling control from her grasp. As he aims the gun at her, Catherine fumbles for the safety catch, her heart pounding.

"You need to take the safety off," Ethan mocks, his voice laced with malice, preparing to deliver the final blow. Suddenly, Bob bursts through the door, rifle aimed at Ethan, triggering a tense standoff. Bullets fly, setting the stage for a clash that will determine Ava's fate.

Amid the clash of bullets and the grim aftermath, Bob's shoulder bears the brunt of a gunshot, while Ethan reels from a strike to the neck. Blood spurts from Ethan's wound, his life slipping away with each passing moment. Catherine, driven by concern, hurries to Bob's side, her face etched with worry as she assesses his injury. In the face of pain, Bob, displaying resilience, offers reassurance, "Could be worse. Check on Cassie."

While Catherine tends to the injured dog, Bob reflects on the harsh reality of their situation. With a touch of grim humor, he acknowledges that a slight difference in trajectory could have meant a dire outcome. Despite the odds, Bob and Catherine prepare to face the challenges ahead, their wounds tended to as best as possible. Bob, undeterred, proposes a plan: "There's a fire lookout tower a mile or so from here.

I reckon our best bet is to head there, see if we can spot it." His voice resonates with determination, a beacon guiding them through the uncertainties.

As they gear up to depart, Catherine's concern extends to Callie, their loyal canine companion who has steadfastly stood by them. She queries, "What about Callie?" Her voice holds a genuine worry for their faithful friend. Meanwhile, the silhouette at the top of the tower remains unmoving, seemingly oblivious to Bob's ascent.

Catherine watches anxiously as Bob navigates the rickety wooden steps, his movements hampered by the gunshot wound. Each creak of the steps becomes a potential signal, and Catherine, hidden behind a tree stump, holds her breath in anticipation. The night, despite its eeriness, remains silent, with only the distant howl of the wind echoing through the surroundings.

Bob persists in his ascent, determined to reach the tower's summit and unveil the truth concealed within its shadowy confines. Catherine, from her vantage point, keeps a vigilant eye on his progress, her heart racing with hope that Bob will reach the top unnoticed.

As Bob inches closer to the pinnacle, his focus unwavering, he faces an unexpected attack from the Masked Man concealed within. A fierce struggle ensues, both men tumbling down the steps in a chaotic melee. Witnessing the brawl unfold, Catherine rushes to intervene, sprinting up the steps to aid Bob. However, by the time she arrives, the Masked Man gains the upper hand, exploiting Bob's gunshot wound to his advantage.

In the midst of the struggle, the air is charged with tension, and the outcome hangs in the balance. Each movement, each blow, is a testament to the stakes at hand. The clash of wills echoes through the desolate tower, surrounded by the mysteries of the night.

The struggle takes an unexpected turn as the Masked Man manages to break free, disappearing into the darkness of the tower. Bob and Catherine exchange determined glances, understanding that their pursuit is far from over. They decide to descend the tower, compelled by the urgency to uncover the enigma and find Ava.

Back on solid ground, the wind howls through the trees, carrying a chilling undercurrent. Catherine looks at Bob, concern mirrored in his eyes. "We can't let them continue whatever dark ritual they're planning," she declares, her voice resolute. Bob nods in agreement, his determination matching Catherine's. "We need to find Ava and put an end to this. I won't let them harm her any longer."

As they traverse the forest once more, their path illuminated only by the occasional flash of lightning, the trees seem to close in around them. Callie, ever loyal, stays close, her senses attuned to the unsettling energies that pervade the woods.

In the midst of the storm, they stumble upon an ancient stone altar, surrounded by twisted roots and ominous symbols. The sight sends shivers down their spines, as if confirming the malevolent forces at play. Catherine's gaze shifts towards a concealed cave entrance nearby. A gut feeling tells her that Ava might be inside, held captive by the mysterious figures conducting the ritual. Bob, trusting Catherine's intuition, nods in agreement.

As they approach the cave entrance, the storm rages on, a symphony of thunder and rain echoing through the forest. The air inside the cave is thick with an otherworldly presence, amplifying the urgency of their mission.

Step by step, they venture into the unknown depths of the cave, the darkness enveloping them like a suffocating cloak. Callie hesitates for a moment but follows, her loyalty unwavering in the face of the inexplicable forces that linger within.

Deeper into the cave, they discover an expansive chamber bathed in an eerie glow. Hooded figures surround Ava, who remains unconscious at the center of an intricate symbol etched on the cave floor. The ritual seems to be reaching its climax, the air heavy with an unsettling energy.

Bob and Catherine exchange a determined glance, silently vowing to rescue Ava from the clutches of the malevolent forces. The hooded figures, oblivious to their presence, continue their chant, their voices merging with the storm outside.

In a desperate attempt to break the ritual, Bob and Catherine move stealthily towards Ava. However, the cave seems to puls.

Witnessing the brawl unfold, Catherine rushes to intervene, sprinting up the steps to assist Bob. However, by the time she reaches them, the Masked Man gains the upper hand, exploiting Bob's gunshot wound to his advantage.

In a desperate attempt to defend himself, Bob fights valiantly, but the Masked Man's onslaught proves overwhelming. With a powerful blow, he propels Bob against the railing, causing it to give way, sending both combatants hurtling through the air.

Catherine watches in horror as they plummet towards the ground, their descent abruptly halted by a sharp tree stump below. Hastening to their side, she gasps in shock at the grim scene unfolding before her.

Bob lies impaled upon the jagged wedge of the trunk, his life ebbing away as he struggles to stay conscious. Beside him, the Masked Man lies motionless, either incapacitated or worse.

With trembling hands, Catherine reaches for Bob's gun, her fingers closing around the cold metal as she aims it at the Masked Man's prone form. Yet, as she prepares to pull the trigger, the Masked Man reveals himself to be a familiar face - Dwayne, a young worker from a local ice-cream parlor.

Paralyzed by disbelief and indecision, Catherine hesitates, unable to bring herself to shoot a child. However, Bob's urgent plea snaps her out of her trance, reminding her of the imminent danger they face.

With a sudden movement, Dwayne produces a concealed gun, prompting Catherine to act swiftly. She fires the rifle, the recoil knocking her off balance as the shot rings out, striking Dwayne with fatal force.

As Dwayne's lifeless body collapses to the ground, Catherine is left stunned by the harrowing ordeal, her senses reeling from the shock of the encounter. With Bob gravely wounded and in dire need of aid, she musters her strength to assist him, determined to do whatever it takes to ensure their survival

Bob's voice was weak as he spoke, his words heavy with resignation. Catherine felt a lump form in her throat, but she fought to keep her composure. She couldn't let Bob see her break down, not now.

""There might be a first aid kit up in the cab," Bob said weakly, his breaths labored and strained.

With a determined expression on her face, Catherine assisted Bob in getting up, supporting him with his arm draped over her shoulder. Together, they struggled towards the steps of the fire lookout tower. Each step was a challenge, but fueled by a glimmer of hope, they pressed on, hoping to find something to patch Bob up and survive.

Finally reaching the top of the tower, Catherine carefully laid Bob down on the platform. Surveying their surroundings, her heart sank at the sight of worn-out equipment and empty drawers scattered with debris.

But then, a ray of hope caught her attention—a first aid kit hung on the wall, untouched. Acting with urgency, she grabbed it and brought it over to where Bob lay.

"I found this," she announced, a touch of optimism in her voice as she opened the kit. However, her optimism quickly faded as she discovered its sparse contents—just a few bandages and some antiseptic wipes.

Bob's condition was critical, his blood staining his shirt as it continued to flow from his wound. Catherine's hands trembled as she applied pressure, attempting to halt the bleeding, but it seemed futile.

"I'm not going to make it," Bob whispered, his voice barely audible in the silence of the night.

""Don't say that. Don't say that," Catherine pleaded, her voice breaking as she locked eyes with Bob. The truth was evident in his gaze—he needed a hospital, and they were miles away from any hope of medical aid.

"I've had a good run. Please sit with me a while," Bob murmured, his strength fading with each passing moment.

With a heavy heart, Catherine nodded, settling down beside Bob. They gazed out over the dark expanse of the forest, the green glow creating an ethereal halo around them. Under different circumstances, it might have been a beautiful sight, but now it served as a haunting backdrop to their impending tragedy.

Catherine's breath caught as she observed the flickering dance of fireflies in the dark forest, their glow resembling ethereal lanterns in the night.

"It's like this place is alive," she whispered, her eyes turning to Bob, her companion in this desperate journey.

Bob met her gaze with a weary expression, a faint smile on his lips despite the pain etched into every line of his face. "It feels that way when the wild wind blows," he replied, his voice hoarse with exhaustion, "but it's just nature. It ain't no spirit. No enlightenment..."

Suddenly, Catherine's attention shifted to a distant glow—a beacon of hope amid the encroaching darkness. "Bob, look," she exclaimed urgently, "over there. A fire!"

But Bob's head had slumped forward, his strength fading with each passing moment. "No no no no no!" Catherine's frantic voice filled the silence as she shook him, desperate to rouse him from the brink of unconsciousness.

Miraculously, Bob gasped awake, his eyes fluttering open as he struggled to cling to consciousness. "Good," Catherine breathed, relief flooding her voice as she clung to the flickering hope that they might yet survive this ordeal, "look, there's a fire. It's got to be them, right?"

With the last vestiges of his strength, Bob lifted his gaze to the distant fire, his voice barely more than a whisper as he directed Catherine's attention. "That's due west of here," he murmured, his words a beacon of guidance in the midst of chaos, "follow the compass. Save your daughter."

Catherine's heart clenched at the thought of facing this perilous journey alone, without Bob by her side. "I can't do this without you," she protested, her voice trembling with fear and uncertainty.

But Bob's conviction remained unshaken, his voice firm despite his weakening state. "Sure you can," he reassured her, a flicker of pride in his eyes as he spoke, "you're a kick-ass London lawyer. You can eat these hillbillies for breakfast."

Tears welled in Catherine's eyes as she thought of Callie, their faithful companion who had been by their side through every trial and tribulation. "What about Callie? She needs you," she pleaded, her voice thick with emotion, "just stay alive a little longer."

But Bob's gaze softened with affection as he spoke of their loyal canine companion. "She'll bring help," he assured her, a wistful smile playing on his lips, "that dog and me... we've been through our share of adventures. Make sure they treat her good once I'm gone."

CATHERINE'S HEART POUNDED in her chest as she stared down at Bob, his once strong frame now weakened by the gunshot wound that stained his clothes crimson. She couldn't bear to leave him, not like this, not when every instinct screamed at her to stay by his side.

"You're not going anywhere," she insisted, her voice trembling with emotion as she clung to the desperate hope that help would arrive in time, "just stay here. Your sheriffs will come looking for us."

But Bob's weary gaze met hers with a sad resignation, the weight of their dire circumstances heavy upon him. "It's too late for that," he admitted, his voice barely more than a whisper as he struggled to draw breath.

Determination flared in Catherine's eyes as she refused to accept defeat, refusing to let despair consume her. "I'm not going to let that happen," she vowed, her voice tinged with defiance as she reached out to him.

A harsh cough racked Bob's body, blood staining his lips as he fought to speak. "Take the rifle and the gun," he instructed, his words strained as he imparted his final instructions, "remember the safety this time. The rifle kicks back, so use your shoulder. There's ammo in the bag."

Catherine's gaze dropped to the ground, her eyes landing on Bob's bag and the rifle lying beside the bloody tree stump. She swallowed hard, the weight of Bob's words sinking in as she realized the gravity of their situation.

"Find them," Bob urged, his voice urgent as he implored her to seek justice, "make them pay for what they took from us..."

A tear rolled down Catherine's cheek as she nodded, her resolve hardening with each passing moment. "I will," she promised, her voice determined despite the tremor that shook her frame.

"Go," Bob urged, his voice growing weaker as he struggled to maintain consciousness, "you can't save me. You can save her."

Catherine's heart ached as she pressed a gentle kiss to Bob's forehead, her tears mingling with his blood as she whispered her farewell. "Go on, now... go..."

With one last lingering look, Catherine tore herself away from Bob's side, her footsteps echoing loudly against the wooden steps as she descended into the darkness below. Bob watched her go, his gaze following her until she disappeared from view, leaving him alone with his thoughts and the encroaching shadows of the night.

In the cover of darkness, Catherine's heart pounds with a mixture of dread and determination as she observes the ritual unfolding before her. She remains hidden among the bushes, her breaths shallow and controlled, her eyes trained on the scene before her.

The fire crackles and dances, casting flickering shadows across the clearing as the masked men move around it in a solemn dance of worship.

Catherine's focus sharpens as she spots the wooden cage holding Ava captive, her daughter bound and gagged inside.

Memories flood Catherine's mind, flashing back to her own childhood trauma, when she was offered as a tribute by her own father. But amidst the chaos of her thoughts, Catherine remains rooted in the present, her instincts urging her to strategize and act with precision.

As she listens in on the conversation between Masked Man #3 and the Masked Leader, Catherine pieces together their plan. Jared and Ethan were meant to lead the sheriff astray while they conducted their ritual. With a sinking feeling, Catherine realizes the danger Ava is in and the urgency of her mission.

With trembling hands, Catherine counts the men gathered around the fire, confirming their numbers. The Masked Leader, now unmasked, reveals a face that Catherine recognizes—the local coroner. Shock courses through her veins as she realizes the extent of the conspiracy that has ensnared her family.

Though fear grips her heart, Catherine knows she cannot falter now. With determination burning in her eyes, she waits for the perfect moment to make her move, ready to confront the darkness that threatens to consume them all.

Catherine's mind races as she listens to Elias's twisted justification for their actions. With a trembling hand, she raises the rifle, her fingers slick with sweat as she struggles to maintain her aim. But the odds are against her—a single shot won't be enough to take down Elias, and there are too many masked men surrounding him.

Realizing she needs a distraction, Catherine's thoughts flash back to a conversation with Zane, where they discussed a strategy of diversion. With determination, Catherine sets her plan into motion. She spots a tall tree nearby with a small hollow at its base, and an idea forms in her mind.

Quickly, she retrieves some bullets from her bag and stuffs them into the hollow along with a bottle of alcohol. Igniting a piece of paper, she drops it into the bottle, creating a makeshift explosive. With a muffled bang, the makeshift bomb detonates, causing the tree to topple towards the fire.

Elias and the masked men are caught off guard as the tree crashes down, sending flames and debris flying. Amidst the chaos, Catherine seizes her opportunity, darting through the smoke and flames to reach Ava, who is trapped in a wooden cage.

With a steady hand, Catherine aims her handgun at the lock and fires, shattering it with a loud clang. She frees Ava from her restraints, tears streaming down her face as she holds her daughter close.

Ava's eyes widen in recognition and relief as she sees her mother. "Mummy!" she cries out, her voice muffled from the gag that has been removed. Catherine gathers Ava in her arms, feeling a rush of adrenaline and fierce determination coursing through her veins. They may be outnumbered, but Catherine will stop at nothing to protect her daughter and put an end to the darkness that threatens their lives.

Catherine's heart races as she and Ava flee through the dense forest, their breaths coming in ragged gasps. With every step, she feels the weight of their pursuers closing in, their shouts echoing through the night.

Suddenly, Ava stumbles over a tree root and falls to the ground. Catherine's heart stops as she watches her daughter tumble to the forest floor, but relief floods through her as Ava quickly picks herself up, tears streaming down her face.

"Ava!" Catherine cries out, her voice a mixture of fear and concern as she rushes to her daughter's side. She takes a moment to assess Ava's condition, relieved to find that she's physically unharmed, albeit shaken and scared.

As Catherine looks up, her gaze falls upon the eerie glow of the enlightenment fire in the distance, casting long shadows over the forest. Silhouettes of masked men dance against the flames, a chilling reminder of the danger they're fleeing from.

Determined to protect her daughter, Catherine steadies herself, recalling Bob's teachings as she lifts the rifle to her shoulder. With a steady hand, she lines up her shot, aiming for one of the masked men in her sights.

Within the depths of the forest, a sharp crack reverberates through the air as Catherine pulls the trigger, the powerful recoil of the rifle surging through her frame. To her astonishment, the masked assailant before her collapses to the ground, incapacitated by her precise shot. Yet, before she can savor the moment of triumph, another shadowy figure emerges from the darkness, their masked visage illuminated by the flickering flames of the fire. With a lethal glint in their eye, they lunge towards Catherine, a gleaming knife poised menacingly in their grasp, poised to strike.

Catherine's heart pounds in her chest as she grapples with the masked assailant, the forest floor slick with mud and leaves beneath them. Desperate to protect Ava, Catherine fights with all her strength, but the masked man gains the upper hand, his knife poised to strike.

In a moment of sheer terror, Ava rushes to her mother's aid, wielding a heavy tree branch with all her might. With a resounding thud, the masked man falls to the ground, unconscious.

Breathless and trembling, Catherine gathers Ava in her arms, their breath mingling in the cool night air as they continue to flee through the darkness. Lost in the labyrinth of the forest, they press on, driven by the fierce determination to survive and find safety amidst the shadows of the night.

THE FOREST CAME ALIVE with the gentle flicker of fireflies, their luminous glow casting a surreal illumination upon the dense foliage. Ava's eyes widened in wonder as she watched the tiny insects dance through the air, their soft light guiding their path.

"They're lighting the way," Ava exclaimed, her voice filled with innocent awe.

Catherine glanced around, her heart racing with a mixture of fear and determination. "I think you're right. Follow me," she urged, her voice steady despite the adrenaline coursing through her veins.

Hand in hand, Catherine and Ava darted through the forest, their footsteps muffled by the thick underbrush. Memories of a similar scene from Catherine's childhood flashed through her mind—a fleeting moment of innocence amidst the chaos of their current predicament.

As they fled through the darkness, the distant rush of water echoed through the trees, a somber reminder of the obstacles that lay ahead. Emerging from the dense foliage, Catherine and Ava found themselves on the banks of the river—a familiar yet daunting sight.

"It's the same river I crossed earlier," Catherine muttered, her gaze sweeping over the wide expanse of churning water. "But there are no stones to jump across. It's too wild to carry us along to safety."

Ava's grip tightened on Catherine's hand, her eyes wide with fear as the sound of approaching footsteps reached their ears. "What do we do, Mommy?" she whispered, her voice trembling with uncertainty.

Catherine's mind raced as she scanned the riverbank, searching for a way to evade their pursuers. Two masked men appeared upstream, their torches casting eerie shadows in the darkness. With a sinking feeling in her chest, Catherine realized they were trapped—surrounded on all sides by Elias and his men.

"Come on," Catherine urged, her voice tinged with desperation as she pulled Ava along the shoreline. Their hearts pounded in unison as they scrambled against the flow of the river, seeking refuge from the encroaching danger.

But their efforts were in vain. Two more masked men emerged from the opposite direction, blocking their path to escape. Elias and his accomplices closed in, their menacing presence casting a shadow over

Catherine and Ava as they huddled together, trapped and defenseless against the encroaching darkness.

THE AIR WAS THICK WITH tension as Catherine stood her ground, her eyes narrowed in defiance as Elias and his masked men closed in on them. Ava clung to her mother's side, her small frame trembling with fear as she watched the menacing figures draw nearer.

"Always causing trouble, wherever you go," Elias sneered, his voice dripping with contempt.

Catherine's grip tightened on the rock she had picked up from the water's edge, her knuckles white with determination. "You stay the fuck away from my daughter," she spat, her voice laced with venom.

But Elias merely chuckled, his masked face contorting into a sinister grin. "She isn't yours," he taunted, taking a menacing step closer. "She belongs to the forest. She's making up for your mistakes."

The rush of the water grew louder, its tumultuous roar echoing through the night as Catherine and Ava edged closer to the riverbank. The sheer force of the current seemed to mock their predicament, threatening to swallow them whole if they dared to retreat any further.

With a fierce determination burning in her eyes, Catherine swung the rock at Elias, aiming for his masked face. But her aim faltered, and the rock sailed past him, missing its mark by inches. Seizing the opportunity, Elias lunged forward, his hands grasping at Catherine's shoulders as he pushed her aside.

With a startled cry, Catherine tumbled into the icy waters of the river, the shock of the cold water stealing her breath away. Elias wasted no time in pouncing on her, his hands wrapping around her throat as he forced her beneath the surface.

"In the early days of the tribute, our ancestors didn't burn them," Elias murmured, his voice muffled by the rushing water. "They took them out into the river, and opened up their bellies, turning the water red."

Desperate bubbles escaped Catherine's lips as she thrashed and fought against Elias's relentless hold, her lungs burning for air. With a final surge of strength, she broke free from his grasp, gasping for breath as she surfaced, her body trembling with exhaustion and fear.

"We burn them now to spread their ashes further," Elias continued, his grip tightening on Catherine's arm. "But I think tonight, we can go back to the old ways."

Ava's anguished cry pierced the night air as she launched herself at Elias, her small fists pounding against his chest in a futile attempt to defend her mother. But Elias easily overpowered her, tossing her aside with a cruel laugh as Catherine struggled to crawl out of the water, her body wracked with coughs as she fought to expel the icy river from her lungs.

AS CATHERINE PLEADED with Elias, her heart pounding in her chest, she saw the glint of the knife in his hand, poised to strike. "Please. Don't. Take me. I'm the one you want," she implored, her voice trembling with fear.

But Elias's masked face remained impassive, unmoved by her pleas. "Not me, Catherine, the forest," he replied coldly. "You had your chance. This is Ava's turn now."

With a sickening realization, Catherine watched as Elias raised his arm, the knife gleaming in the moonlight. She was helpless, paralyzed with fear as she braced herself for the inevitable.

But then, a sudden rush of sound cut through the air, the sharp bark of a dog echoing across the water. Startled, Elias turned just in time to see Callie hurtling towards him, her powerful jaws snapping at his wrist.

With a cry of pain, Elias dropped the knife, his arm falling limp at his side as Callie latched onto him, her teeth sinking deep into his flesh. Catherine wasted no time, rushing to Ava's side and pulling her away from the chaos unfolding before them.

The masked men, their guns trained on Callie, hesitated, unwilling to risk hitting Elias in their attempt to subdue the ferocious dog. In that brief moment of hesitation, floodlights suddenly illuminated the scene, casting a blinding glare across the river.

It was the cavalry, led by Sheriff Brad Tucker, who had arrived just in time to intervene. "This is the Teton County Sheriff's department. Place your weapons down and your hands up," Brad's voice boomed through the car speakers, commanding authority.

Caught off guard, the masked men hesitated, their resolve faltering in the face of the overwhelming force arrayed against them. With a sense of urgency, they turned and fled into the forest, disappearing into the darkness.

But Elias remained, his voice filled with desperation as he watched his followers abandon him. "No, where are you going. We need to offer the tribute!" he cried out, his words echoing across the river as he was left alone, his grip on power slipping away.

LEFT ALONE ON THE RIVERBANK, Elias's desperation drove him to pick up the knife with his remaining good hand, his eyes wild with fervor as he advanced towards Catherine and Ava, who trembled at the water's edge. "I have to do it. You don't understand what will happen if I don't," he muttered, his voice tinged with desperation and madness.

Across the river, Sheriff Brad Tucker observed the tense standoff, his gaze focused intently on the unfolding scene. "You got a clear shot," he called out to his deputy, only to receive a negative response. "Stop right there. Do not go any closer," Brad commanded through the car speakers, his voice carrying authority and urgency.

Catherine and Ava watched in horror as Elias approached them like a spectral figure, his intentions clear and menacing. "The world will end," he muttered ominously, his voice a chilling whisper that sent shivers down their spines.

Suddenly, a helicopter appeared overhead, its spotlight illuminating the scene with blinding intensity. Elias faltered momentarily, his eyes wide with fear as the unexpected intrusion startled him. Sensing an opportunity, Catherine seized the moment, her adrenaline-fueled resolve propelling her into action.

With swift determination, she lunged forward, grabbing the knife from Elias's hand and driving it into his chest with all her strength. Elias's eyes widened in horror as he staggered backwards, his body convulsing in agony as he was overcome by a rush of pain.

With a final, guttural gasp, Elias toppled backwards into the raging river, his body swept away by the powerful currents. The helicopter's spotlight followed his descent, casting an eerie glow over the water as his lifeless form collided with the jagged rocks below, staining the river red with blood.

Meanwhile, the helicopter shifted its spotlight to the forest, tracking the fleeing masked men as they attempted to escape into the darkness. On the ground, more sheriff's deputies emerged from the shadows, their torches casting long shadows as they surrounded the surrendering fugitives, their reign of terror coming to a decisive end.

Seated in the car, Catherine and her daughter Ava shared a moment of somber tranquility, the events of the day casting a heavy pall over their spirits.

Catherine and Ava clung to each other at the water's edge, their tears mingling with the soft lapping of the river as they finally allowed themselves to release the pent-up fear and tension that had gripped them throughout their harrowing ordeal. The bitter taste of blood and smoke still lingered in the air, a haunting reminder of the violence that had surrounded them.

As the sun dipped below the horizon, casting a warm glow over the scene, the sound of approaching sirens shattered the tranquility of the moment. More sheriff and police cars rolled onto the scene, accompanied by a couple of ambulances. Paramedics rushed to tend to

Ava, guiding her gently into one of the ambulances where a paramedic carefully examined her for any signs of injury.

Meanwhile, Catherine sat just outside the ambulance, her fingers absentmindedly stroking Callie's fur as she waited for any news. Sheriff Brad approached her, his expression somber as he spoke.

"Ms. Wilson, how are you and Ava holding up?" Brad inquired, his voice laced with concern as he took in the exhausted faces of the mother and daughter.

Catherine nodded, her throat constricted with emotion as she struggled to find the words. "Did you find Bob?" she asked, her voice barely above a whisper as she awaited confirmation of her worst fears.

Brad nodded solemnly, his gaze dropping to the ground in recognition of the sacrifice made by his fallen comrade. "He was a hero," Catherine murmured, her voice thick with emotion as she spoke of the man who had given his life to protect them.

"That he was," Brad agreed, his voice tinged with sadness as he acknowledged Bob's bravery in the face of danger.

Catherine's attention returned to Callie, who whined softly at the mention of Bob's name, her loyal companion sensing the weight of their loss. Brad reached out a comforting hand, offering his support as they navigated the aftermath of their traumatic experience.

"They're going to take you to the hospital," Brad informed her, his voice gentle as he guided Catherine through the next steps of their journey to recovery.

As the scene unfolded around them, a montage of the aftermath played out in Catherine's mind. She and Ava were checked out by a doctor at the hospital, their injuries tended to with care and precision. Brad's voice echoed in her ears, reassuring her that they would do everything possible to ensure their well-being in the days to come.

After enduring the tumultuous events that had unfolded, Catherine found herself confined to a hospital bed, the sterile white walls of the room offering a stark contrast to the chaos she had recently faced. Brad, along with an FBI agent, stood at her bedside, their questions probing into the details of the recent ordeal. Catherine recounted the events as best she could, her voice wavering as she relived the terrifying moments that had threatened to consume them.

"I'll need to pop in at some point to get your statement. I imagine others might have questions too," Brad's voice echoed in Catherine's mind as she nodded in response, her mind already racing ahead to the next steps in their journey to safety.

Days passed in a blur of hospital visits and interviews, until finally, Catherine and Ava were deemed fit to leave. With weary hearts but a renewed sense of hope, they collected their belongings from the hotel where they had taken refuge during their ordeal.

"And then we'll get you safely on your way back to the UK," Brad's reassurance lingered in Catherine's thoughts as they loaded their bags into the trunk of the rented SUV parked outside the hotel. Ava's voice broke the silence as she questioned their next steps.

"Are we going home now?" Ava's eyes held a mixture of uncertainty and longing as she looked to her mother for reassurance.

Catherine nodded, offering a small smile of reassurance. "Yes, we just need to do one more thing and then we'll head to the airport," she replied, her voice tinged with exhaustion but determination.

With a final glance around the familiar surroundings, Catherine closed the trunk of the car, sealing away the memories of their tumultuous journey as they prepared to embark on the final leg of their journey.

The small chapel of the crematorium stood bathed in soft sunlight as Catherine and Ava stood side by side, surrounded by the solemn silence of mourning. A local funeral celebrant conducted the service, offering words of comfort and solace as they paid their respects to Catherine's father.

Sheriff Brad stood respectfully at the back of the chapel, a silent sentinel of support as Catherine and Ava bid their final farewells to their beloved patriarch.

As they emerged from the chapel into the crisp daylight, the celebrant accompanied them, presenting Catherine with a small urn containing her father's ashes. With heavy hearts but a sense of closure, Catherine and Ava accepted the urn, their steps faltering slightly under the weight of their grief.

Together, they walked away from the crematorium, their journey marked by the bittersweet memories of loss and resilience, but also the enduring bond of family and the unwavering support of those who had stood by their side through it all.

Brad is waiting for them at his sheriff's car in the small car park. CATHERINE: Thank you for coming. You didn't have to. BRAD: I don't think Bob would have forgiven me if I hadn't. Besides, someone wanted to say goodbye. Brad opens his car door. Callie paws out of the car and immediately comes to Catherine and Ava. CATHERINE: What's going to happen to her? BRAD Think she's earned her retirement. Her and Bob served together since she was a pupper. Catherine strokes Callie's soft fur, looking into her big brown eyes. CATHERINE: Thank you. Both of you. BRAD: We should be thanking you. Whole town owes you a debt. You have a safe flight. CATHERINE We will. Catherine and Ava go to their SUV, as Bob and Callie watch.

Catherine and Ava embarked on their final drive through Jackson, savoring the sights one last time before merging onto the highway.

Their rented SUV cruised effortlessly along the expansive stretch of highway, traversing through a lush forest that enveloped them in a tranquil embrace. As they neared a bridge that spanned over a spirited river, Catherine eased off the accelerator, guiding the vehicle to a halt before pulling over to the roadside.

"You wait here. I'll be back in a moment," Catherine instructed, clutching the urn containing her father's ashes before exiting the car, her footsteps echoing softly against the asphalt.

Outside, Catherine walked halfway across the bridge until the roaring river flowed beneath her feet. Closing her eyes, she immersed herself in the wild wind swirling around her.

Memories flooded her mind in a rapid succession:

- Bob's voice echoing from the fire tower, speaking of the wild wind.
- A young Catherine holding a gun, Joseph guiding her from behind.
- The red wine stain on her kitchen wall in London.
- Elias staggering into the river, the water turning crimson.
- Zachery's question haunting her in the law office.
- Catherine firing the rifle at the fire tower, the recoil sending her sprawling as Dwayne fell, his face maimed.
- Young Catherine aiming at a buck in the forest, fear and excitement mingling in her eyes as Joseph urged her to shoot.
- Catherine freeing Ava from the wooden cage at the enlightenment fire.
- Ava's terrified scream at the ice cream parlor.
- Young Catherine watching her father chasing them down the street.
- Ava and Catherine running through a dark forest illuminated by fireflies.

The scene changed smoothly from the montage. It showed a flashback of young Catherine lying in the peaceful forest, her breathing matching the gentle movement of the trees.

Returning to the present, Catherine stood upon the bridge, her chest rising and falling in synchrony with the memory of her younger self. With her eyes tightly shut, she surrendered to the rhythmic pattern of her breath, allowing herself to be carried away by the currents of nostalgia and introspection. Amidst the quietude, the untamed whispers of the wind intertwined with her steady inhalations and exhalations, weaving a tapestry of serenity that enveloped her in a moment of profound contemplation.

Catherine stood resolute upon the bridge, her gaze unwavering as it traced the relentless flow of the river beneath her. With a deliberate and steady hand, she cradled the urn containing her father's ashes, its weight heavy with memories and emotions. As she delicately unsealed the vessel, a gentle breeze whispered through the air, carrying with it the essence of her father's being. With a solemn reverence, she poured the ashes into the wind, watching as they danced and twirled in graceful arcs, each particle a testament to a life well-lived. In the embrace of the golden sunlight, the ashes glistened like ethereal particles of stardust, painting the surface of the water with a shimmering mosaic of memories. It was a sad and sincere goodbye to a loved parent, a moment remembered forever as proof of the strong connection between a father and his daughter.

Several days later, Catherine and Ava found themselves nestled in the confines of an aircraft, homeward bound. As the airplane commenced its journey down the runway, Catherine's heart danced with a symphony of emotions—anticipation mingled with a hint of trepidation. The aircraft surged forward, its engines roaring to life, causing a subtle tremor to reverberate through the cabin. Ava, initially gripped by a palpable sense of unease, instinctively clutched onto her seat for stability. However, in a poignant moment of unity and vulnerability, she reached out for her mother's hand, intertwining their fingers with a resolute grip. Touched and profoundly moved by this spontaneous display of connection, Catherine felt a surge of pride welling within her, tears of admiration and affection glistening in her eyes as the plane ascended gracefully into the boundless expanse of the sky.

Amidst the tranquility of the night, Catherine observed Ava nestled peacefully beside her, headphones in, lost in the embrace of sleep. Beyond the window, a faint glow emerged on the horizon, steadily intensifying with the advent of dawn. As the sun ascended, its radiant beams brushed the clouds with delicate shades of pink and lilac, casting a serene aura over the scene. A wave of tranquility enveloped Catherine, a sensation she had yearned for since the trials they had endured. Gazing affectionately at her daughter, she couldn't help but smile, appreciating the beauty of Ava, flaws and all, in her slumber.

Back in the comforting glow of her kitchen at home, Catherine sat before her laptop, engaged in remote work for a non-profit organization dedicated to the noble cause of locating missing children.

Catherine's attention was drawn to her screen as an email notification from her former boss, Grant, materialized. Intrigued, she clicked to open it, revealing a link to a BBC News article detailing the latest developments concerning Zane and his father, Zachery. The headline delivered the definitive news of Zane's incarceration for manslaughter. A mixture of emotions stirred within Catherine: a faint sense of satisfaction washed over her, acknowledging that justice had been duly served, and a wave of relief swept through her, grateful that she was no longer obligated to defend him.

With a gentle click, Catherine shut her laptop, signaling the end of her work session. Descending the stairs, Ava appeared, engrossed in cheerful conversation on her iPad with John and her newborn brother, Felix. Ava extended the device to Catherine, who accepted it, listening intently as John inquired whether Ava would be interested in spending the Easter break with them in Switzerland. Glancing at Ava, Catherine observed her daughter shaking her head with a resolute gesture.

Catherine's face brightened with a smile as she concluded her conversation with John, gratified that Ava had accepted the invitation to join them in Switzerland. Turning to her daughter, who regarded her with curiosity, Catherine remarked, "You should meet your brother."

Ava shrugged, acknowledging the validity of her mother's statement. "I suppose you're right."

"Would you like to take a stroll?" Catherine suggested.

Ava's eyes sparkled with excitement. "Can we grab some ice cream?"

Catherine chuckled softly. "But it's winter."

"That just means it'll stay cold longer," Ava reasoned.

"I see your point. Callie! Let's go for a walk," Catherine called out, beckoning their furry companion to join them.. Callie, Bob's loyal German Shepherd who had become a part of their family, padded into the kitchen. Catherine attached a leash to her collar, and they set off from the house.

Outside, Catherine, Ava, and Callie made their way towards a tree-lined path leading to town. The wind whispered through the branches as they walked, a peaceful scene as they embarked on their journey together.

THE END